MURIEL'S MURALS
The Adventure Of Beaufort Primary School

Written by Dean Wilkinson
Illustrated by Rebecca Morton

First published in 2016
Text copyright © Dean Wilkinson 2016
Illustrations copyright © Rebecca Morton 2016
Dyslexie font created and copyrights © Christian Boer

Lexie Mouse Design
72a Pope Lane, Penwortham,
Preston, Lancashire,
United Kingdom PR1 9DA

www.lexiemousedesign.co.uk

Printed in the United Kingdom by B & D Print Ltd
www.bdprints.co.uk

Dedicated to my husband, Richard Morton, and my daughters, Ruby and Scarlett.
Rebecca Morton

Thanks to all at Beaufort Primary School, especially Tina Nowell and Keith Gibson
for being good sports. Cheers to all the children and Rowena Sisterson for her
'colouring in'!
www.beaufort.surrey.sch.uk
Thanks too to Joanne Kitching for her rabid editing skills.

HEARTFELT NOTE FROM DEAN WILKINSON :
A huge thanks to Dave Vanian and Captain Sensible from The Damned for words of
encouragement when I needed them most. Your inspired anarchy and musical genius
has spurred me on for 40 years; long may it continue. 'Bazzazz' comes from a
misheard lyric from White Rabbit.

www.deanwilkinson.net

Visit Muriel's website www.murielsmurals.com

The font used in this book was created by Dr Christian Boer of
Dyslexie Font B.V. and designed to make reading a less arduous task.

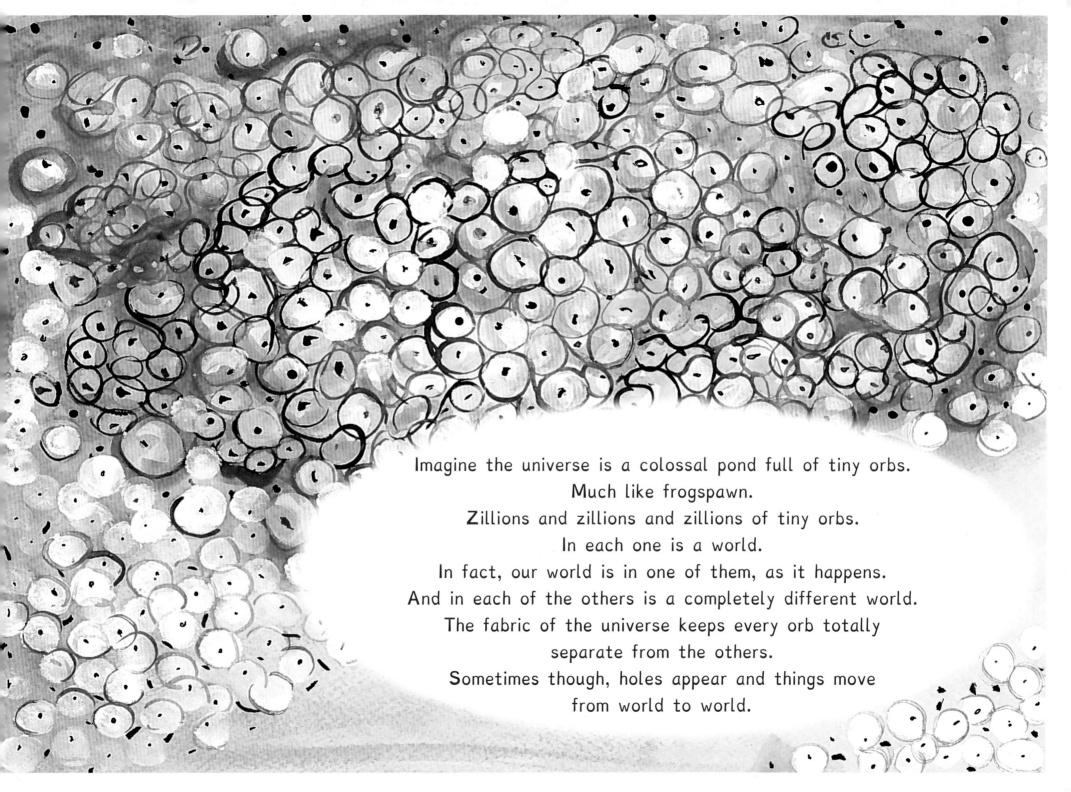

Imagine the universe is a colossal pond full of tiny orbs.
Much like frogspawn.
Zillions and zillions and zillions of tiny orbs.
In each one is a world.
In fact, our world is in one of them, as it happens.
And in each of the others is a completely different world.
The fabric of the universe keeps every orb totally
separate from the others.
Sometimes though, holes appear and things move
from world to world.

SCHOOL

In another orb is the dark world of Bazzazz.
There are some horrible things in Bazzazz that
want to get into our world.
Why? To create chaos and spoil stuff.
Creatures like Tommyrots, Snoodles, Wazzocks,
Blitherers, Skellingtones,
Mimsy-Pipsies, and countless more.

CHOOL

Luckily, our world has ways
of defending itself. One
such way is Kitsch-Witches.
Clever, creative and magical
people who have ways of
rounding up these terrible
creatures and sending them
back to Bazzazz.
Muriel is a Kitsch-Witch
and these are her stories.

The Adventure Of Beaufort Primary School

'Thank goodness you're here, Muriel!' said Mrs Nowell, the Head Teacher of Beaufort Primary School. She was frantic as she greeted Muriel at the entrance of the school.

'Calm down, dear,' said Muriel reassuringly. 'You've had some supernatural visitors during the night, hey? Relax, I can sort it out.'

It was a bright, warm, early summer morning. Muriel pushed her bike into the school reception. Her saddlebags were crammed with paints and brushes and goodness knows what else. In the basket on the handlebars was her sidekick and familiar, Dali, an anteater. He nodded at Mrs Nowell as if to say, 'Morning'.

'How did you hear about me?' asked Muriel.

'Mrs Casson from The Neil Armstrong Primary mentioned you in a blog about a year ago. Of course, we all thought she was madder than a wardrobe full of cheese. She was wittering about weird and spooky creatures rampaging in her school, but now I believe her!' replied Mrs Nowell.

'Oh yes, nasty business,' mused Muriel. 'A couple of hundred Skellingtones doing a conga line down the corridor as I remember. They took some shifting I can tell you!'

Mrs Nowell showed Muriel to the Main Hall and the damage the intruders had done the previous night. There were chairs and tables thrown about. Books, papers, smashed plant pots and other debris was all over the floor. It looked like teenagers had had a party there, and then some more teenagers had come in and had another party.

Mrs Nowell knew it couldn't have been burglars as all the windows and doors were still locked tight. She'd double-checked because Mr Gibson the caretaker was away on holiday, so it was down to her to secure the school.

Dali bounded out of the basket and began examining the mess. His finely tuned nose sniffed the air and he eyed the terrible scene carefully.

Muriel dropped to her knees and moved her left eye ever so closely to the floor. She stayed like that for a few moments. Her head then jerked up and she lapped at the air like a puppy licking your hand. She put her tongue away and nodded knowingly.

What they were both checking for was anyone's guess, but they obviously knew exactly what they were doing.

'Definitely a Grade 4 break through. Wazzocks is my guess, or Blitherers, but let's let the Time Catcher prove it,' said Muriel gleefully. She clearly enjoyed her job.

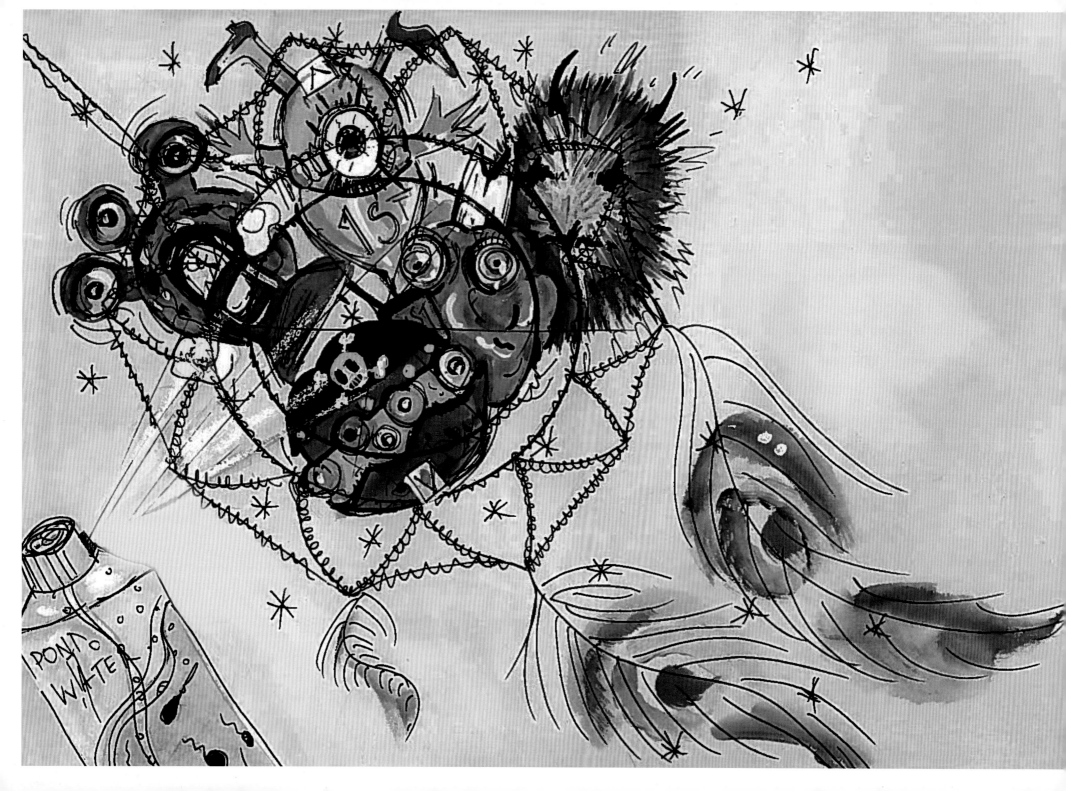

Muttering a spell to herself, Muriel sprayed a kind of dream catcher contraption with terrible smelling water from a bottle. A moving image appeared in the Time Catcher. It was a short recording of events from the night before. It showed some odd looking little creatures running riot in the hall. They threw anything they could get hold of, and seemed to have enormous strength and mindless, directionless energy.

'Knew it. Wazzocks. Pretty routine job,' giggled Muriel. 'Although you'll need to cancel school today. Tell the kids it's a boiler-breaking-down day. They'll be most pleased.'

'I've already had the secretary ringing around telling the parents and carers,' said Mrs Nowell.

She stared at the image in the Time Catcher that played a few seconds of what had happened over and over again. 'What are...Wazzocks?'

Muriel looked up at Mrs Nowell. She smiled nicely and said, 'All in good time dear. First, I need to see your lost property box.'

'Wazzocks are from a world called Bazzazz. They're like a terrible, violent bacteria that lives to spoil things. It's what they do. You can't reason with them,' said Muriel as she pulled shirts, shorts, socks and odd shoes from the smelly lost property box.

'Bazzazz? Is that another planet?' asked Mrs Nowell, as a pair of muddy socks landed on her head.

'Yes and no. It's all to do with dimensions and stuff like that. The universe is home to an infinite amount of invisible worlds, but they're usually quite separate from one another. Sometimes though, holes appear in dark, unpleasant places – like at the bottom of lost property boxes. That's when things move around. Unwelcome things.'

Mrs Nowell was amazed to see that the bottom of the box was a window to another world. The world of **Bazzazz**. A shady and scary woodland with eerie, shadowy creatures lurking in the dark. It was like watching something on a TV screen. There was just the normal world around the box, but inside the box was a view of a strange and different place. She felt quite giddy at the sight.

'This portal's still open. Ho ho, you're lucky you haven't had a stampede of Wazzocks, Skellingtones, Mimsy-Pipsies and goodness knows what else,' chuckled Muriel. She sprayed the smelly water into the box.

'Oh my stars! I had no idea there was so much else going on in the universe!' gasped Mrs Nowell. 'And I thought parents' evening was mad!'

'Bazzazz!' said Muriel and the portal closed. The box became a box again.

'We'd better get you some Mural security guards to protect your school in case this happens again. My Murals are magic and have ways of dealing with anything beastly that might break through from **Bazzazz**. Of course, they'll need to track down the Wazzocks that are already here. Wazzocks sleep through the day in the most ingenious places, so we will never find them. We need to be prepared for tonight when they wake up.'

Mrs Nowell gulped. 'You mean they're still here?'

'Paints and brushes at the ready, Muriel,' said Dali as Muriel and Mrs Nowell came back into the Main Hall. Dali had laid out a selection of paintbrushes and different coloured paint tins ready for inspection by his Kitsch-Witch boss.

'I guessed the Murals you'll be painting here today - one Banksy the fox, one Constable the penguin and one Jackson the elephant. And definitely three of those annoying monkeys.'

'Spot on, Dali,' said Muriel with a big beaming smile.

'Did that anteater just talk?' gasped Mrs Nowell.

'No, you're hearing things, deary. Must be your age,' said Dali dryly.

'Oh well, that's a relief,' replied Mrs Nowell with a hint of sarcasm, 'We wouldn't want anything weird to happen in the school.'

She turned to Muriel. 'So while you're painting your Murals, Muriel, what should I do?'

'I have a vital job for you, dear. Stick the kettle on and make us all a nice cup of tea,' chuckled Muriel with a big grin.

Muriel got to work painting her Murals. With well-practised hands, her brushes guided the paint onto the wall. Jackson The Elephant began to take shape.

Dali and Mrs Nowell watched more of the Wazzocks' antics from the night before. Dali had asked Edison to scan the atmosphere for more detailed information about the invading Bazzazzers.

Edison was a kind of magic computer that could read invisible clues left in the air, which Dali called Event Sparks. He explained to Mrs Nowell that Event Sparks stay in the atmosphere for a very long time after something dramatic or unusual happens. Like making footprints in wet concrete.

'Okay, you have six Wazzocks. They are Captain Terrible-might have known he'd show his face again. Shadrack, don't know him. Flob, she has a sweet tooth so she'll be asleep in the kitchen somewhere. Me-Me, she's new. Snarky-ooh, I can't stand Snarky! Oh, and his sister, Narky. Nasty little things,' said Dali as he read the long paper text tape coming from Edison.

'What's the smelly water for?' asked Mrs Nowell, wincing as she sniffed the sprayer.
'It's Pond Water that at least 50 frogs have swum in because frogs are enchanted.
I don't want to scramble your brain with culture shock by explaining the true nature
of reality, but frogs, kind of, well...created...everything,' explained Dali.
Mrs Nowell was about to reply but decided there was only enough weirdness she
could handle in one day.
'A splash of Pond Water on anything makes it vulnerable to spells. It oils the magic
cogs, so to speak. We have to spray each of the six Wazzocks with the stuff to
send them back to Bazzazz.'
Mrs Nowell looked sick with concern. 'But what if they come back when you're not
here to spray them?' she gulped.
'Once the Murals are completely dry, they have their own ways of dealing with
intruders from Bazzazz. Trust me, with Muriel's Murals standing guard, your school
will be 100% safe,' Dali reassured her. Then added under his breath, 'Ish.'

The day went by quickly. Mrs Nowell did her best to tidy the school whilst Muriel and Dali finished the Murals. A huge elephant, a serious looking fox, a friendly looking penguin you felt you could trust, and three cheeky monkeys that seemed charged with boundless energy.

Outside the sky became dark and the moon appeared.

When in the human world, Wazzocks wake up at night. It wouldn't be long before they'd emerge from their slumber and embark on that night's wrecking spree. And that's when Muriel, Dali and the Murals could deal with them. Potentially, it could get quite dangerous so Muriel advised Mrs Nowell to go home and leave them to their task. The Head Teacher didn't need telling twice and they soon heard her car wheels spinning out of the school gates.

Suddenly, there came a loud and terrible wailing, crashing and musical cacophony from the music room. The first of the Wazzocks had woken up!

'Wake up!' yelled Muriel as she sprayed Jackson with the Pond Water.
The elephant twinkled with magical light, opened his eyes and looked around.
'Music room. Wazzocks. Go go go!' yelled Muriel excitedly.
As quick as a flash, and moving like a film projector's image on a screen,
Jackson slid down the wall, onto the floor and out into the corridor heading
towards the music room. He left spatters of paint in his wake.
The game was on!

In the music room, the Wazzock called Captain Terrible had switched on all the electric guitars and keyboards at full blast. He punched holes in tambourines, bent triangles straight, and snapped recorders and flutes before throwing them at the guitar strings. He danced madly, stamping hard on the keyboard keys. The din was deafening. He sang loudly and tunelessly as he trashed the room sounding like some deluded X-Factor contestant.
Jackson slid into the music room and onto the ceiling. When he was above Captain Terrible he let himself go and fell like a ton of paint onto the wretched little Wazzock.

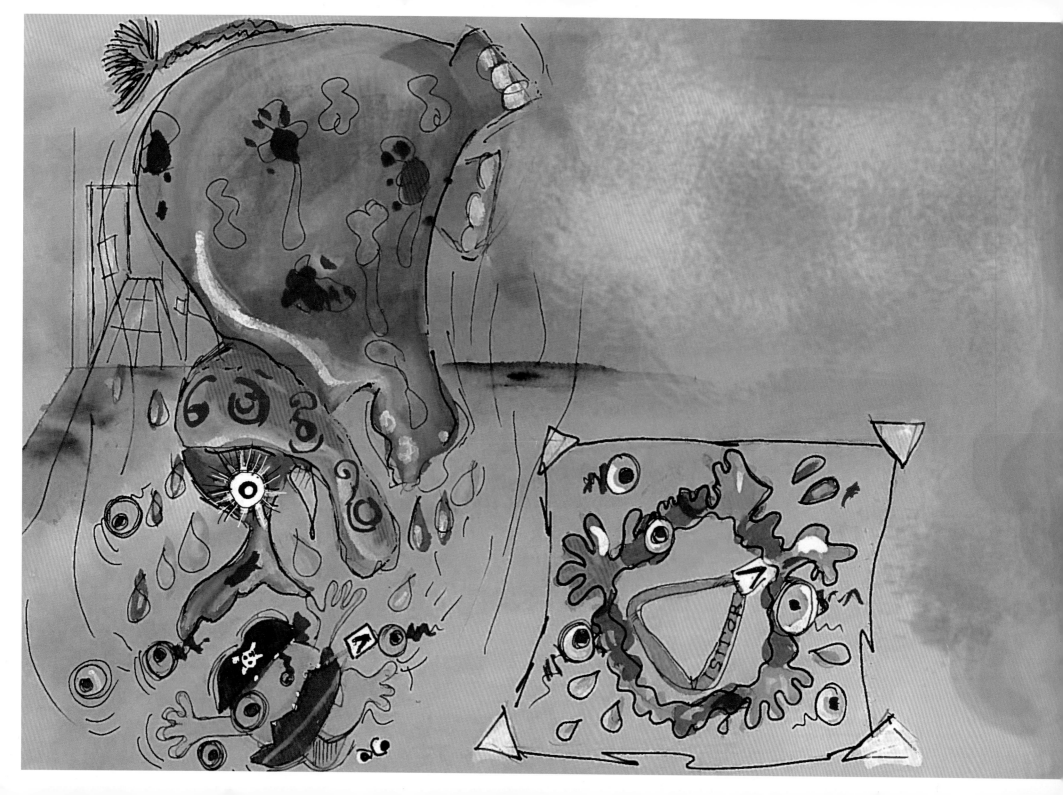

Spladoosh! Jackson knocked Captain Terrible out cold. Paint splashed everywhere like a multi-coloured tidal wave! Jackson rose up out of the paint and reformed his shape on the music room wall. He eyed the unconscious Wazzock daring him to move.

Muriel ran in and sprayed the Captain with Pond Water. The Wazzock instantly awoke and his eyes bulged at the sight of her.

'Taxi for Terrible,' said Muriel playfully. 'Next stop Bazzazz!'

In a bright, colourful flash the first Wazzock was gone, back to its own world.

The Wazzock named Flob was rampaging in the kitchens looking for any cakes, chocolate or sugar to eat that she might have missed the night before. What a sticky, gooey mess she was making! Flour, margarine, milk and cooking oils were strewn about the place like a mad, cookery-inspired collage.

Flob was searching for something sweet, but what was about to happen to her couldn't be candy-coated.

Banksy the fox was cold and stern. He never cracked a smile. He could move as fast as lightning and had snuck inside a cupboard in the twinkle of an eye.

Flob tore open the cupboard door and didn't even have time to yelp at the sight of the paint fox lunging out at her with his mouth wide open. In an instant, Banksy had Flob clamped in his teeth!

The stealthy fox shook the frantic Flob from side to side so hard and fast her eyes were out on stalks and her tongue was lashing about like a flag in a gale. Dali walked in and viewed the scene.

'Flob, Flob, Flob! How many times do we have to go through this? Too many sweets will rot your teeth. You'll notice how strong Banksy's are?'

Flob couldn't have answered if she'd wanted to as she was so utterly disorientated. She didn't know whether she was coming or going. She was actually going-back home!

'That's because Banksy brushes with minty white Bazzazz!' said Dali as though he were in a TV toothpaste advert.

Banksy dropped the exhausted Wazzock onto the floor and Dali sprayed her with Pond Water.

With a colourful flash, Flob was gone. Dali and Banksy nodded their approval at one another. A most satisfying bit of teamwork.

Shadrack, an incredibly spiteful little Wazzock, was busy in the library moving all the books out of alphabetical order. This would make them so much harder to find. He was going to tear out the last few pages from every book so no one would ever know what happened at the end of each story. He really was as unpleasant as something an overpaid premiership footballer blows out of his nose on the pitch.

As he worked, he glanced up and noticed a picture of a penguin on the wall that he hadn't seen the night before. Shadrack was puzzled because normally he noticed everything!

Shadrack was right to be curiously concerned as the picture was Constable the penguin. With an almighty leap, the paint penguin tore himself from the wall and onto Shadrack. This knocked the wind out of the grim Wazzock-and a loud bottom burp too! Faaaaart!
Paint from Constable splattered everywhere. The penguin flipped the Wazzock onto his front and slapped a pair of multi-coloured paint handcuffs around his wrists.

Constable had arrested Shadrack and was taking him to Muriel. The vile little Bazzazzer was unrepentant and blew wet raspberries and spat greenies all the way there.
Muriel, the judge and jury, dealt with him swiftly. In an instant, the dire Wazzock was magically deported back to Bazzazz. Justice was served and not a moment too soon!

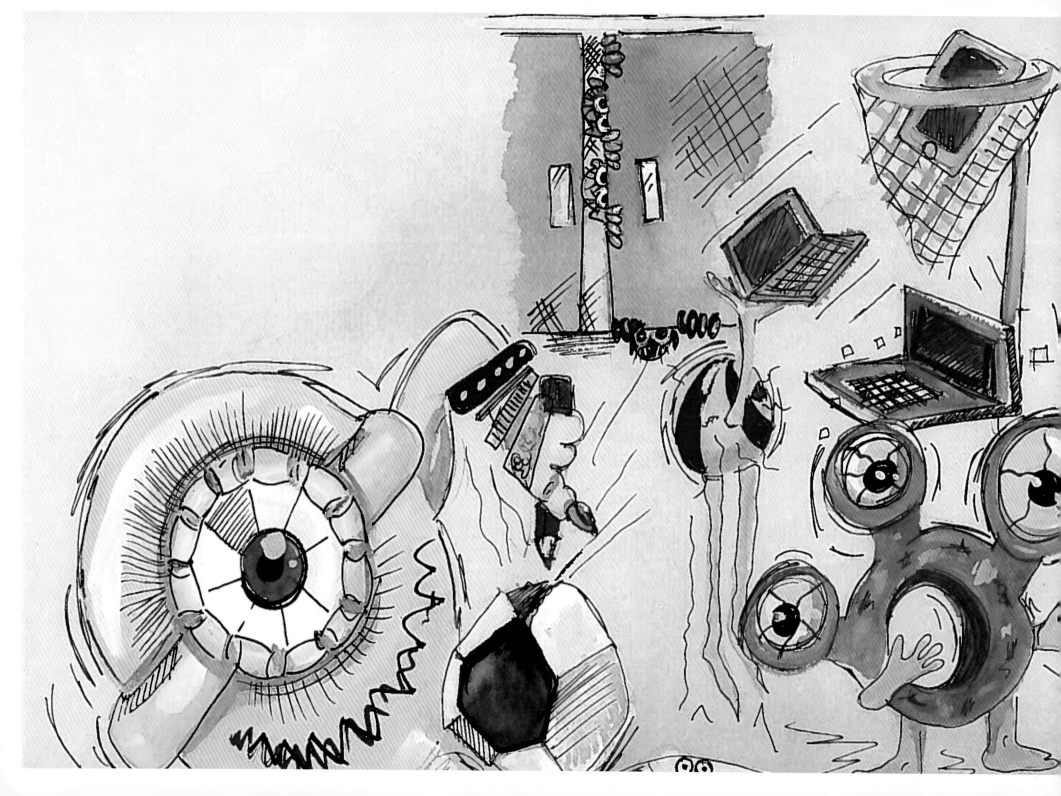

The last three Wazzocks were in the Sports Hall. Me-Me was popping footballs with a sharp pencil. Snarky and his sister Narky were having fun playing 'electronic basketball'. This involved throwing all the school's iPads, laptops and other electronic devices through the basketball hoops. They cackled madly as each device smashed when it hit the floor.

The three paint monkeys, Magritte, Monet and Miro, peered in through a crack in the Sports Hall doors. They had their prey in their sights.

In an extraordinary display of acrobatics, the monkeys threw the remaining Wazzocks around like rag dolls. The paint simians chucked, caught, dropped and snatched them in mid-air and every direction. It was quite a show.
The grand finale came when Muriel and Dali sprayed a large cloud of Pond Water into the air and the monkeys tossed each of the Wazzocks into it.
The instant each Wazzock passed through the smelly water vapour, Muriel and Dali sang 'Bazzazz! Bazzazz! Bazzazz!'
Each of the Wazzocks vanished in three bright flashes, sent home where they could do no more harm in the human world.
Job done! Well, almost.

Just then, Mr Gibson, the school caretaker, ran into the Sports Hall. He lived on the school grounds and had just got back from his holidays, arriving by taxi. Seeing the lights on in the school, he'd rushed in to investigate and found the school in a terrible mess. Huge puddles and splashes of paint were everywhere. That was shocking enough, but now he was looking at a witch, an anteater and several moving Murals on the walls of the Sports Hall! It was simply too much for him, especially after his long flight home, and he fainted on the spot!

After a pause, Muriel said, 'He's going to need another holiday to get over this.' Both she and Dali burst out laughing.

It was clean-up time. Dali was about to set the Paint Splatter Spiders to work eating up all the splashed paint around the school. He opened their tins and hundreds of them scurried out.

Made from living paint, there were three kinds of magical spider: red, blue, and yellow. They went about their work at amazing speeds, gobbling up every last drop of mixed paint and transforming it to a primary colour.

In a matter of minutes, the school was paint-splash free. The spiders, now fatter and full, darted back to their tins.

Muriel and Dali then set about undoing the damage the Wazzocks had caused.

It was quite a task repairing the smashed school equipment. They used spells and enchantments to return furniture, books, pens, pencils, musical instruments and everything else back to its rightful place and in perfect working order. In some cases better than before-the computers and laptops now loaded in seconds - if you can imagine that!

Muriel and Dali had left by the time the children and staff started to arrive the next morning. Pupils and teachers alike were amazed at the brand new Murals on the walls.

Thanks to Mrs Nowell's kindness and a nice cup of tea*, Mr Gibson eventually got over the shock of what he'd seen. He put it down to jet lag and the dodgy meal he'd eaten on the aeroplane.

To this day, the Beaufort Primary School has been Wazzock-free. Mind you, if any Bazzazzer ever did break through they wouldn't last long. Not with Muriel's Murals standing guard ready to pounce on them and Bazzazz them back home!

THE END

*A nice cup of tea is actually an old magic 'calming' spell and works as a remedy for most upsetting events.

ABOUT THE CREATORS OF MURIEL'S MURALS :

REBECCA MORTON

Rebecca has been designing sets for TV and film for over 20 years. Her very first job was model building and set dressing on the iconic kids show, Teletubbies.

Soon after her first daughter was born, Rebecca had a sudden impulse to paint a seaside scene on her nursery wall. Before long, the walls and even the furniture were painted to look like sand dunes or rock pools and the ceiling was a blue sky dotted with fluffy white clouds! She soon turned her compulsion for bringing walls to life into a successful business and has been commissioned to paint many large murals, especially in schools. Rebecca is married to stand up comedian and composer Richard Morton and is the proud mum of daughters Ruby and Scarlett.

DEAN WILKINSON

Dean is a television scriptwriter, novelist and games writer. He was Ant and Dec's writer for seven years, penning the multi-award winning SMTV Live & Chums.

He wrote two series of his own CBBC sitcom, Bad Penny, starring Graham Fellows (aka comedian John Shuttleworth), as well as two series of his CBBC sketch show, Stupid.

For games, he has written for the entire LittleBigPlanet series, Fantasia: Music Evolved, Driver San Francisco, Worms and many others.

His long career has seen him scribbling for Stephen Fry, Hugh Laurie, John Cleese, Smith & Jones, Matt Berry, Simon Pegg and Harry Hill to name drop but a few.

Dean Earle Wilkinson is a proud father to three daughters, Emily, Alice and Grace.

www.deanwilkinson.net